# Remy and Lulu

Written and
illustrated by

## Kevin Hawkes

With miniatures by

## Hannah E. Harrison

Alfred A. Knopf
New York

THIS IS A BORZOI BOOK PUBLISHED BY ALFRED A. KNOPF

Text, jacket art, and full-sized illustrations copyright © 2014 by Kevin Hawkes
Miniature illustrations copyright © 2014 by Hannah E. Harrison

Visit us on the Web! randomhouse.com/kids

Educators and librarians, for a variety of teaching tools, visit us at
RHTeachersLibrarians.com

*Library of Congress Cataloging-in-Publication Data*
Hawkes, Kevin.
Remy and Lulu / written and illustrated by Kevin Hawkes ; with miniatures
by Hannah E. Harrison. — 1st ed.
    p.   cm.
Summary: A down-on-his-luck painter with poor eyesight teams up with
a dog with a knack for painting portraits.
ISBN 978-0-449-81085-9 (trade) — ISBN 978-0-449-81087-3 (lib. bdg.)
[1. Artists—Fiction. 2. Dogs—Fiction. 3. Portraits—Fiction. 4. Vision—
Fiction.] I. Harrison, Hannah E., ill. II. Title.
PZ7.H31324Rem 2014
[E]—dc23
2012021740

The text of this book is set in 15-point Goudy Old Style.

MANUFACTURED IN CHINA

September 2014

10  9  8  7  6  5  4  3  2  1

First Edition

To Sean,
a great artist
—K.H.

To Kevin Hawkes,
with immeasurable gratitude
—H.E.H.

Lulu lived in the studio of a great portrait painter on the Rue de Rivoli
in Paris. Every day she studied, and watched. She was very hardworking.
And very smart.

One day, the studio was sold and all the beautiful portraits were
packed into crates and taken away in a wagon.

Lulu wandered the city, sleeping in doorways, eating from trash bins.

She followed a road that took her far into the countryside.
There under a fig tree she met a man with a tangled mop of hair.
Beside him lay an easel, some rolls of canvas, and a paint box.

"*Bonjour!*" he said. "My name is Remy. Would you care for
some lunch?"

They shared a lump of hard cheese, a stale crust of bread, and
some figs.

"What shall I call you?" Remy asked. He squinted at the collar
around her neck.

"Lulu?"

She wagged her tail.

Remy was a painter. He traveled around the countryside painting portraits.

He preferred large canvases and liked to use bold colors straight from the tube.

"I paint the essence of a person, not their likeness," he explained to Lulu.

"My eyesight is not good," Remy joked, "but my vision is clear!"

Lulu noticed that few people were willing to pay for "essence."

When Remy painted, Lulu sat at his feet. He was like a wild man, snorting, grumbling, attacking the canvas with brushes full of dripping paint.

One day, in the middle of a portrait of Madame LeGrosse, Remy had to stop. His hands trembled and his head ached. He and Lulu had not eaten in three days. He went outside to rest under a tree.

Lulu picked up a brush, squinted her eyes, and went to work.

Later that afternoon, Remy finished the painting. He was out of breath and pale.

"*Voilà*," he said weakly.

Madame LeGrosse frowned at the portrait. Monsieur LeGrosse's face became very red. He opened his mouth. Remy closed his eyes and braced himself.

"Ooh la la!" exclaimed Madame LeGrosse suddenly as she bent over. "*Chéri*, look! Such detail! Such color!"

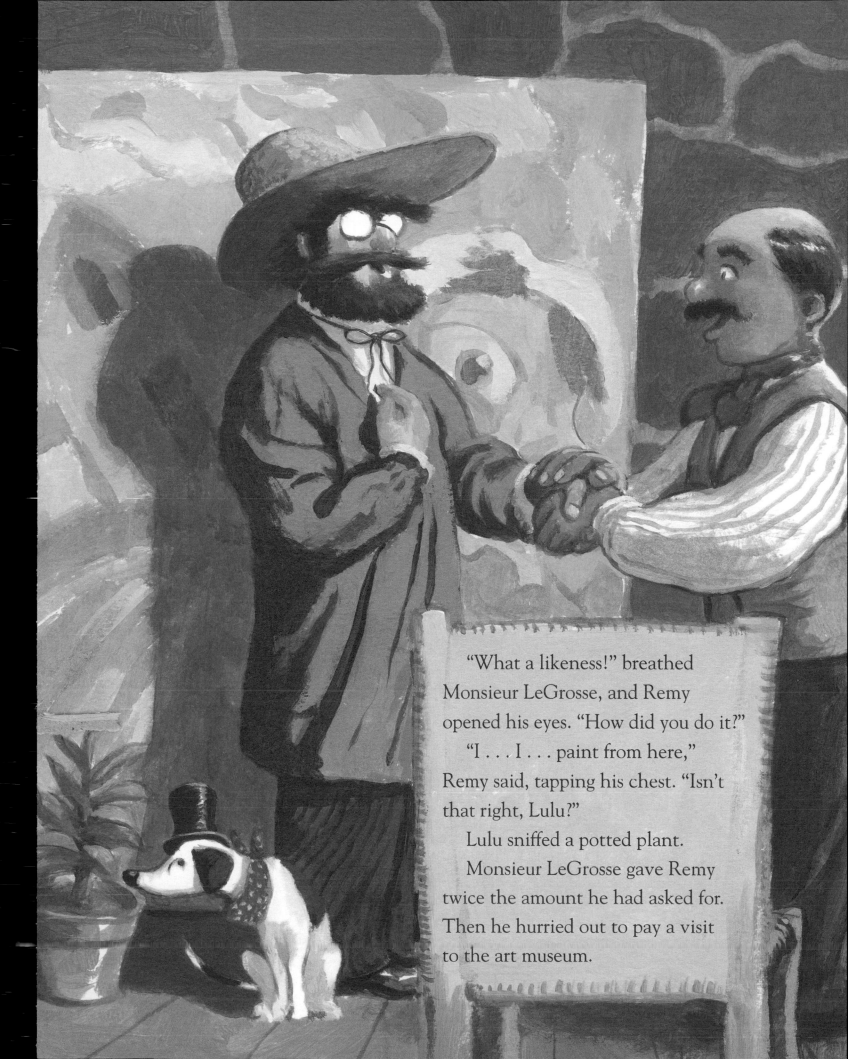

"What a likeness!" breathed Monsieur LeGrosse, and Remy opened his eyes. "How did you do it?"

"I . . . I . . . paint from here," Remy said, tapping his chest. "Isn't that right, Lulu?"

Lulu sniffed a potted plant.

Monsieur LeGrosse gave Remy twice the amount he had asked for. Then he hurried out to pay a visit to the art museum.

Later that night, while feasting on sausage and pâté, Remy laughed.
"You see, Lulu!" he cried. "When you follow your heart, success will
follow *you*!" Lulu thumped her tail and ate another piece of sausage.

From then on, Remy and Lulu were very busy. Remy painted portraits of doctors, lawyers, musicians, even Mademoiselle Gigi, the famous actress. Everyone wanted a portrait by Remy.

They rented a fine studio on the Rue de Rivoli. Remy bought a top hat and a silk scarf. Lulu wore a different silk handkerchief every day. There were parties to attend and picnics in the park. There was always enough to eat.

Remy's next portrait was of the famous optometrist Doctor Lunette. It was to be entered in the Salon, the most prestigious art contest in all of Europe. He worked day and night on the large canvas.

"So, what do you think?" he asked Lulu. Her tail thumped against the Oriental carpet.

At the Salon, the judges were astonished.

"Such detail!" they cheered. "Such color!" they cried.

"We award the gold medal to Remy!"

Remy and Lulu danced for joy!

"Please!" interrupted Doctor Lunette. "As a token of my appreciation, I should like to present you with a little gift."

"Ooh la la!" whispered Remy as he tried on the silver-rimmed spectacles. For the first time, he noticed the color of Lulu's eyes. He gazed at the crowd, the good doctor's smiling face, and the finished portrait.

"Such . . . detail," he wondered, scratching his beard.

"Such . . . color," he murmured, glancing at Lulu, who
sniffed the edge of the carpet.

"A perfect likeness . . ." He frowned.

They rode home in silence.

After that, the paint on Remy's palette became hard
and dry. Patrons came, but Remy turned them all away.
Lulu tried to cheer him up. She performed her favorite
tricks, but he only shrugged his shoulders and looked out
the window.

One day, Lulu brought him an envelope that had been slipped through the mail slot.

It was an invitation from Madame Renard, the owner of the exciting new Galerie Renard. She wanted to meet him and Lulu and have a portrait done. Could they please come the next day to her château in the countryside?

Remy read the letter twice and rubbed his chin thoughtfully. He remembered the sun on his face, the wind in his hair, and the taste of figs.

The next morning, Lulu was surprised to see Remy standing at the door. He had on his old painter's smock and his straw hat. He stood with his paint box in one hand and some rolls of canvas in the other. He smiled for the first time in days.

"Lulu," he said. "I have been missing the fresh air of the country and the sunshine. I think this will be our last portrait. Eh? Then we shall paint landscapes in the country, perhaps. *Non?*"

Lulu's ears drooped.

Remy nodded. "I understand. Once a portrait painter, always a portrait painter."

"I have something for you," Remy said. "If a
painter has her own vision, then she should have
her own tools."

The carriage ride was long. When at last they stepped down
at the gate, Remy breathed in the fresh country air and sighed.
They walked up the long path together.
"What fantastic shapes!" murmured Remy. "Such detail!"

Madame Renard met them at the door.

"My dear Remy!" She smiled. "It is so good to finally meet you." He offered his hand.

"And this must be Lulu, whom I have heard so much about!" She leaned over to pat Lulu on the head. "Please do come in." She led them down a long corridor filled with paintings.

Remy very cautiously touched the brush to the canvas. He began to paint ever so slowly. First his eyes focused on Madame Renard's striking hat. Then he studied the exquisite diamond necklace that hung around her neck. He noticed the folds in her dress, the red leather boots, the complicated patterns in the Oriental rug. His eyes darted from one detail to the next, like birds fluttering from twig to twig. His brush hesitated, unsure which way to go.

Lulu studied the small square of canvas on her easel. It was quiet. Too quiet.

At last, Remy shook his head.

"It is no use. I am sorry, Madame Renard," he said. "But I cannot . . ."

He felt a tug at his pant leg and looked down. Near his foot, on the rug, was a bundle. Lulu nudged it toward him with a paw.

Remy unwrapped it. He stared for a moment at the old familiar glasses. Then he smiled and put them on his nose.

He peered toward Madame Renard, who waited patiently. He took a deep breath, squinted his eyes, and, with a laugh, attacked the canvas. His feet swished on the carpet as he paced. His hands jumped here and there, and the brush smacked the canvas, which quickly filled with bold, thick brushstrokes.

Lulu painted quietly. The only sound she made was the thump, thump, thump of her tail on the floor.

*"Voilà!"* Remy announced several hours later. "The portrait is complete!"

When Madame Renard saw the painting, she gasped.

"It's perfect," she said. "A perfect essence! How do you do it?"

Remy blushed. "I paint from here!" he said, tapping his chest.

After examining Lulu's painting
with a special magnifying glass,
Madame Renard clapped her hands.
"Genius!" she cried. "Pure
genius! You must display your
work in my gallery!"
Remy smiled. Lulu
wagged her tail.

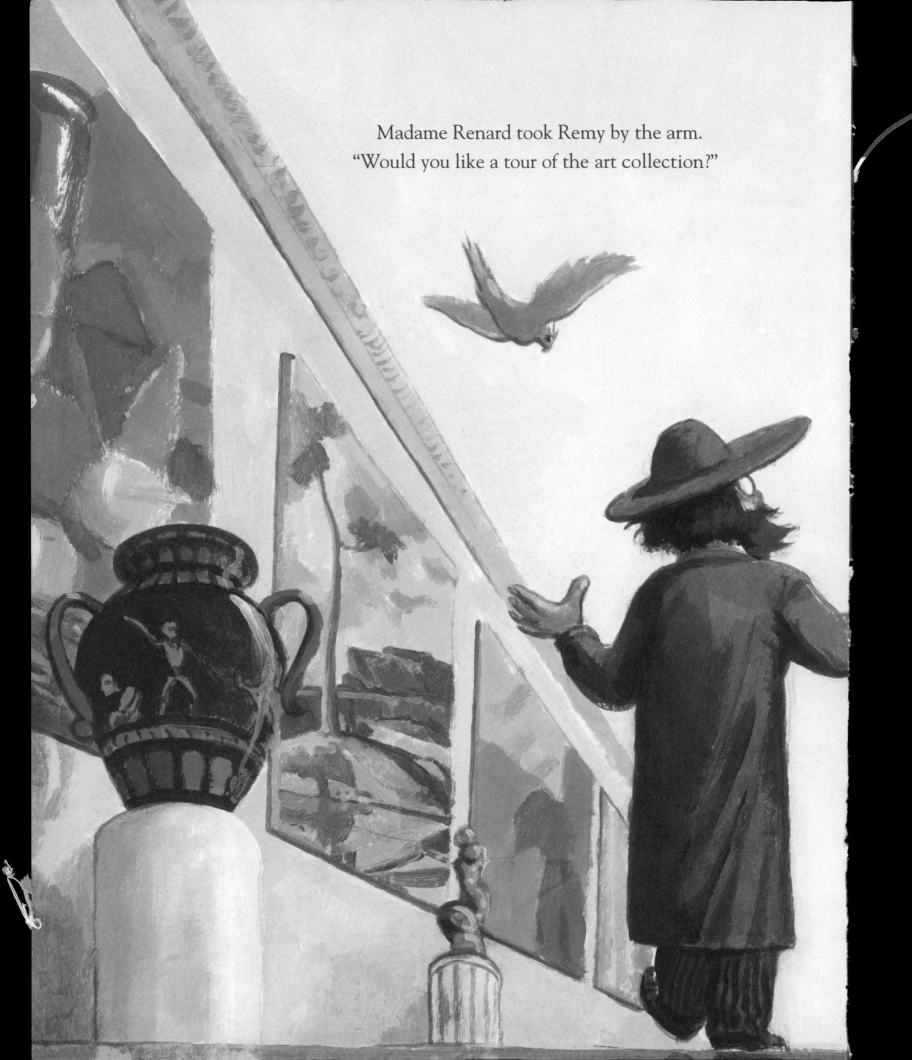

Madame Renard took Remy by the arm.
"Would you like a tour of the art collection?"

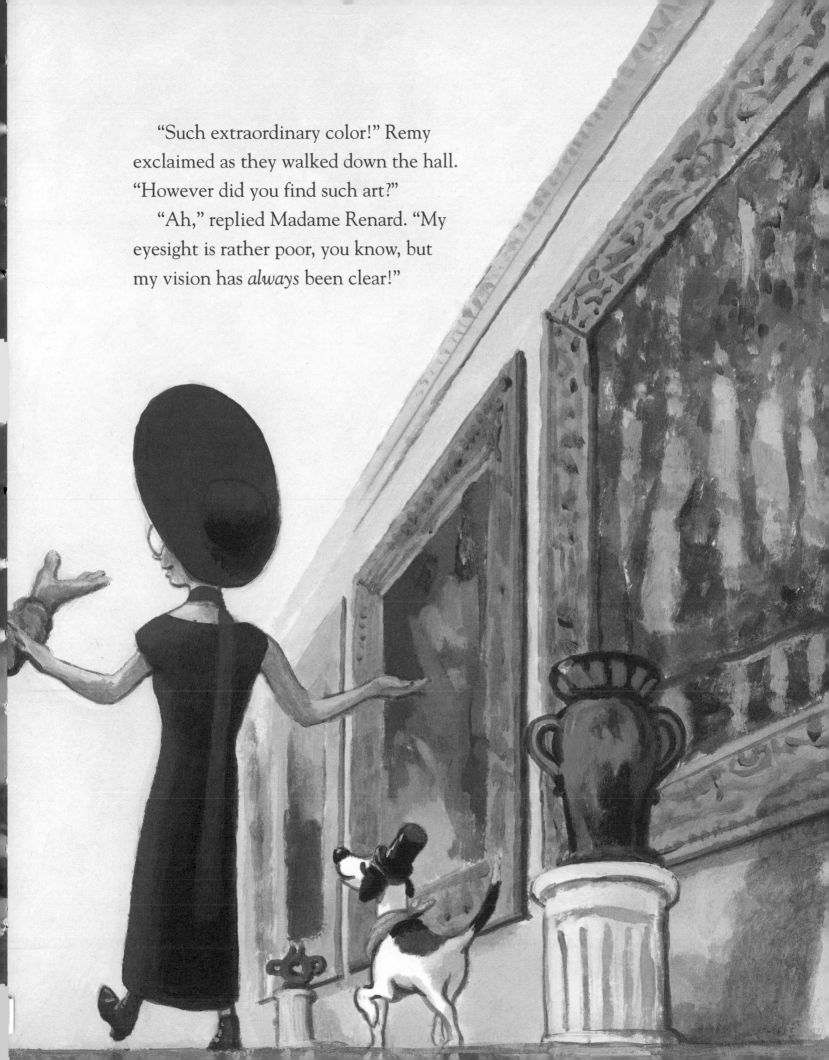

"Such extraordinary color!" Remy exclaimed as they walked down the hall. "However did you find such art?"

"Ah," replied Madame Renard. "My eyesight is rather poor, you know, but my vision has *always* been clear!"